Magic
Animal Friends

For Kitty Hinds, with love

Special thanks to Valerie Wilding

ORCHARD BOOKS

First published in Great Britain in 2016 by The Watts Publishing Group

1 3 5 7 9 10 8 6 4 2

Text copyright © Working Partners Ltd 2016
Illustrations copyright © Working Partners Ltd 2016
Series created by Working Partners Ltd

A CIP catalogue record for this book is available from the British Library.

ISBN 978 1 40834 122 3

Printed in Great Britain

MIX
Paper from
responsible sources
FSC® C104740

The paper and board used in this book are made from wood from responsible sources

Orchard Books
An imprint of Hachette Children's Group
Part of The Watts Publishing Group Limited
Carmelite House, 50 Victoria Embankment, London EC4Y 0DZ

An Hachette UK Company
www.hachette.co.uk
www.hachettechildrens.co.uk

Amy Snowycoat's Daring Dive

Daisy Meadows

ORCHARD

Map of Sapphire Isle

Bubbling Brook

Bucket and Spade
Shop

Prettywhiskers'
Purrfect Ice Cream
Parlour

Shimmer Lake

Admiral Greatwing's
House

To
Grizelda's
Tower

Can you keep a secret? I thought you could!

Then I'll tell you about an enchanted wood.

It lies through the door in the old oak tree,

Let's go there now - just follow me!

We'll find adventure that never ends,

And meet the Magic Animal Friends!

Love,
Goldie the Cat

Contents

CHAPTER ONE

To Sapphire Isle!

"Nearly finished!" Lily Hart said, shaking water from her hands.

She and her best friend, Jess Forester, were planting reeds at the edge of a pond they'd been building. It was near the Helping Paw Wildlife Hospital, which Lily's parents ran in a barn in their

 9

garden. Both girls adored animals, and loved spending their spare time helping at the hospital.

Some of the patients were watching from nearby pens. A little fox cub sat with her head on one side, and two fluffy bunnies woffled their noses as they peeped at the girls.

"Ducks and frogs will love the pond," said Jess.

"Insects, too!" She smiled as a shimmering blue dragonfly perched on a lily pad that was drifting across the pond. "It looks like it's having a ride!"

Lily grinned. "Like we did when we floated on giant lily pads to Sapphire Isle!"

Sapphire Isle was in a secret place called Friendship Forest. The girls' friend, Goldie the cat, had taken them on lots of amazing adventures there. It was a magical world where the animals could talk! They lived in little cottages and met their friends in the Toadstool Café to drink honey and raspberry smoothies.

"I hope we go back to Friendship Forest soon," Lily said. Then she spotted something moving in the reeds. A flash of golden fur!

Out stepped a beautiful green-eyed cat.

"Goldie!" the girls cried.

She curled around their ankles, purring. Then with a quick glance up at the girls, Goldie darted towards Brightley Stream at the bottom of the garden.

"Come on, Lily!" said Jess. "We're going to Friendship Forest!"

They raced after Goldie, across the

 12

stream's stepping stones, into Brightley Meadow.

"Maybe Grizelda's causing trouble again," said Lily.

Grizelda was a horrible witch who wanted to drive all the animals away from Sapphire Isle, so she could build a holiday tower and have the island all to herself.

As Goldie reached a dead-looking tree in the middle of the meadow, it burst into life, sprouting scarlet and gold autumn leaves. Fluffy red squirrels hunted for seeds in brown cones, while tiny wrens sang joyfully among the branches. In the grass below, golden dandelions turned their faces to the autumn sun.

The girls caught up as Goldie touched the trunk. Two words appeared in the bark.

Lily and Jess held hands tightly and read aloud, "Friendship Forest."

A door with a leaf-shaped handle appeared in the tree! Jess opened it, letting golden light spill out.

Goldie bounded inside and the girls followed. They felt the familiar tingle that meant they were shrinking, just a little.

As the light faded, Jess and Lily found themselves in a forest glade, surrounded by trees.

Candyfloss flowers and orange-scented daisies nodded in the soft, warm breeze.

And there was Goldie, standing upright, wearing her glittering scarf. But she looked worried. "I'm so glad you're back in Friendship Forest," she said in her soft voice.

Jess held her paw. "What's wrong?"

"Has Grizelda stolen the last sapphire?" asked Lily.

The witch had already stolen three of the four magical sapphires that protected Sapphire Isle. The first one was guarded by the Prettywhiskers cat family. It kept Shimmer Lake at the right temperature. The Paddlefoot beavers guarded the second one, which kept the water clean. The third, which kept the lake calm, was guarded by Millie Picklesnout the piglet's family. The girls and Goldie had managed to get the sapphires back, but Grizelda always had horrible new plans

for making trouble.

"She hasn't stolen the sapphire yet, but I'm worried she will," said Goldie. "Today's Sapphire Isle Swimming Gala. She'd love to ruin it."

The girls hugged her. "If she does, we'll do our best to stop her," said Jess.

"We must hurry and check the sapphire's safe," said Goldie.

She took the girls along a narrow path towards Shimmer Lake. At the shore they found Mr Cleverfeather, the elderly owl, waiting on a very funny-looking boat. It was shaped like a huge nest with a big hooter on the front. It had three funnels, painted red, blue and green. Mr Cleverfeather was wearing a jaunty striped sailor's hat as well as his usual waistcoat and monocle.

"Hoo yoo!" he called, muddling his words as usual. "I mean yoo hoo! This way for Sapphire Isle! Dep on steck!"

Lily giggled. "He means step on deck."

As the boat chuffed along, its funnels puffed out coloured smoke that matched their paint.

Jess sniffed. "The smoke smells like peppermint!" she said.

When they were close enough to
see the island's harbour village and
grassy hills, they noticed lots of animals
splashing around near the shore.

"They're practising for the races,
I expect," said Goldie.

Lily's eyes shone. "The swimming gala's
going to be so exciting!"

CHAPTER TWO

Danger in the Water

Mr Cleverfeather lowered the gangplank onto a beach that was dotted with rockpools.

"All ashore," he said. "Don't pep in the stools – I mean, step in the pools!"

Goldie, Jess and Lily climbed down. "Thank you!" they called, as Mr

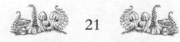

Cleverfeather's boat chuffed away.

The girls peered into the nearest rockpool, and laughed in delight when a crab looked up and waved his claw. In the next pool, a circle of rosy starfish danced around a sea anemone, while shrimps played hide and seek among the seaweed.

"Come on! We must check the fourth sapphire is safe," said Goldie. They headed towards a pretty cottage, decorated with coloured shells. It was surrounded by a moat, with a narrow wooden bridge leading to a door. Stacks of armbands, floats

and rubber rings were piled outside. Some were tiny enough for a mouse, and others were big enough for the girls. A sign said, "Snowycoat Swimming School".

"The Snowycoats guard the fourth sapphire," Goldie was saying, when an adorable little white face popped up from

 23

the moat. It had huge dark eyes, and was

wearing a sparkling tiara!

"A seal pup!"

cried Lily.

The seal

wriggled out

of the water

and shook

droplets from

her fluffy white

fur. "I'm Amy

Snowycoat," she said. "It's so lovely to

meet you! I help teach swimming in

Shimmer Lake with my dad."

 24

"Wow!" said Jess. "You must be a great swimmer."

The seal pup smiled shyly. "Goldie told us how you saved three of the Shimmer Lake sapphires. I'm glad you're here," she added quietly. "Will you help my family?"

Jess stroked Amy's white fur. "Yes, if we can," she said.

"Thank you. Please come inside," said Amy. "I'll see you there." She dived back into the moat.

The friends crossed the bridge, went into the cottage and stared in surprise. One side of the house had a floor with

 25

thick blue carpet and a long green sofa.
The other side was a pool, with a raft
and floating furniture, like big, soft,
squishy bubbles.

Amy popped out of the water, making
them jump. She climbed onto a floating
sofa. "We Snowycoats never use the
door," she said. "We have our own way in,
underwater!"

Suddenly, a big seal shot out of the
water onto the raft. He wore a red sun
visor, and was followed by a tiny white
seal pup wearing a yellow bib.

"Hi, Dad," said Amy. "Goldie's brought

Jess and Lily to help us."

"Welcome!" said Mr Snowycoat, while
the tiny seal pup climbed up to snuggle
with Amy.

She put her flipper around him. "This is
my little brother, Jack."

The girls noticed a small red rubber
ring bobbing on the water. In it was a

lovely blue shell. Jess and Lily had seen
ones like that before.

"Is your sapphire inside that shell?"
asked Lily.

"Yes," said Amy. She scooped it up and
opened it. Inside was a glittering blue
heart-shaped sapphire. It sparkled in the
sunlight shining through the window.

"It's beautiful!" Jess said.

"It keeps the lake at the right level,"
said Mr Snowycoat. "But its magic only
works if the sapphire's in its shell."

"That's why we need help," said Amy.
Her glistening dark eyes were huge.

"We're worried that Grizelda will steal our sapphire while we're at the swimming gala."

"That's easy," said Jess. "Lily and I will look after it."

Mr Snowycoat clapped his flippers. "Wonderful!"

Jack clapped his little flippers, too. "Fufful!" he said, copying his dad.

Amy gave the sapphire in its shell to Lily, who tucked it safely in her pocket.

"Right!" said Mr Snowycoat. "Off to the gala!"

As they crossed the beach, the Snowycoats didn't go around the pools like everyone else. They pulled themselves over the sand with their flippers and when they came to a rockpool, they slipped into the water and glided sleekly across it.

Soon they reached a cove that was bright with green and yellow bunting. Animals stood around, chatting. Some of them spotted the girls and shouted, "Hello!"

Jess and Lily
waved to Amelia
Sparklepaw the
kitten, whose
blue swimsuit
matched her
eyes. Lola
Velvetnose the
mole looked cute

in a pair of goggles instead of her usual

huge spectacles, and the Longwhiskers

bunnies hopped with excitement.

Coloured flags marked out swimming

lanes and a diving area, and a row of

gold medals lay ready on a table.

When Mr Snowycoat climbed onto the podium, all the animals rushed to sit on deckchairs and rugs. Goldie and the girls settled on the sand to watch the fun.

The backstroke race was first. Jess and Lily noticed that the smallest creatures, such as mice, hamsters and voles, were allowed to start a little way in front.

Mr Snowycoat raised his whistle.

"Ready?"

Peeeeep!

The race began with lots of excited

squeaks. Poppy Muddlepup took the

lead, then Lottie Littlestripe the badger

streaked past. But as she overtook Olivia

Nibblesqueak the hamster, the water swirled and began to churn!

Lily and Jess gasped as Olivia was swept out of the swimming lane, but she managed to hang on to a squirrel's bushy tail.

The animals squealed in fright as they struggled to shore. The Snowycoat seals, the Paddlefoot beavers and the Slipperslide otters were in the water in a flash, helping everyone to safety.

A screechy noise, like a rusty trumpet, blasted out from underwater. Then a flag with a cauldron and crossed brooms rose from the lake. A funnel appeared next, draped with slimy seaweed.

Jess gasped. "Grizelda's steamboat! She's magicked it to go underwater, like a submarine!"

Once the boat had surfaced, the tall, bony witch appeared from a hatch. She wore a purple top over skinny black trousers and high-heeled pointy boots, and her green hair whipped around her head.

"Haa!" she cackled. "The interfering girls and their meddlesome cat!"

She glared at Amy. "Who's this fluffy-flippered creature?" She laughed. "If you lot think you'll spoil my plans," she screeched, "think again!"

The four friends looked at each other in horror.

Amy's dark eyes brimmed with tears. "She's ruining everything!"

Jess hugged the little seal. "We've stopped her wicked plans before, Amy. We'll do our very best to stop her again!"

CHAPTER THREE

Imps on the Run

The animals huddled behind the low wall at the top of the beach.

Lily patted her pocket. The sapphire was safe as long as the witch didn't know where it was.

"Go away, Grizelda!" Jess yelled. "There's nothing for you here!"

"There is!" shrieked the witch. "My servants will find it!" She stamped her foot. "Imps! Get that sapphire!"

The girls recognised the four small creatures who leapt from the hatch. Their skin was blue and they wore tattered

trousers and stripy tops, like little pirates. There was Kelp, with his wooden

leg, and his seaweed net. Greedy Urchin
was gobbling a slimy green sandwich.
Barnacle had her thumbs tucked in her
shiny-buckled belt, and little Shrimp still
wore his yellow armbands.

"Arr, me hearties!" cried Kelp, leaping
into the water. "Let's find the jewel!"

Urchin swam ashore and ran to the
nearest picnic. She stuffed a huge bun into
her mouth, finishing with a loud "Burp!"

The girls watched, dismayed, as
Barnacle and Shrimp joined Kelp,
zooming about the beach.

"Sapphire!" Grizelda shrieked. "Now!"

But Shrimp spotted the medals. "There be gold!" he cried, grabbing them.

As Kelp passed the Snowycoats, he swung his net and scooped Jack up.

"Dadda!" the tiny seal pup squeaked.

Amy threw herself at Kelp. "Leave him alone!" she cried.

Urchin squealed with laughter. "Fluffy be trying to stop Kelp! Fluffy hasn't got a chance!"

"Maybe not!" cried Jess. "But she *has* got friends!"

She grabbed Kelp's net, untangled Jack and bundled him into Lily's arms.

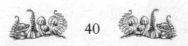

Suddenly, Barnacle shouted. "There be the jewel!"

Lily glanced down. To her horror, the sapphire shell was poking out of her pocket.

She passed Jack to Goldie, but before she could escape, Barnacle shoved her into the water.

Splash!

The shell fell out of Lily's pocket and floated away!

"Get it, you lot!" Grizelda screeched.

Urchin, Barnacle and Kelp leapt into the water and swam after the shell.

Barnacle grabbed it and opened it. Urchin took out the sapphire, and they tossed the empty shell aside.

"Ahoy, Shrimp!" shouted Kelp. "Time we be gone!"

Shrimp turned around, clutching fistfuls of medals. "These be too shiny to leave to landlubbers," he said, leaping

into the lake.

Lily tried to follow them but they dived underwater, taking the sapphire with them.

Jess spotted the shell in a patch of floating seaweed and waded out to get it.

Grizelda shrieked with laughter. "That empty shell's no use, you silly girl!" she crowed. "Watch the lake!"

Water was creeping up the beach.

"Oh, no!" cried Goldie in dismay. "Now the sapphire's out of the shell, its magic has stopped!"

The water level was rising, fast!

"Haa!" Grizelda cackled. "This flood will wash the animals' homes away! First from the island, then the whole forest! And when the water level

goes back down, I'll build my holiday tower right here. I'll have Sapphire Isle *and* Friendship Forest all to myself!"

She disappeared belowdeck. With a screechy blast from the funnel, the slimy steamboat slipped beneath the waves.

The animals crept out of hiding.

"The lake's flooding!" cried Mrs Scruffypup.

The deckchairs and rugs were already

submerged, and water lapped the wall
at the top of the beach. The little animals
were scurrying away as fast as they could,
but the lake was already swirling around
their paws.

"It'll reach the cottages soon," Jess said
to Lily. "We must get that sapphire back,
but first, the animals need help."

Amy and her dad gave armbands and
rubber rings to anyone who couldn't
swim. "Move your legs like this," said
Amy, showing them with her flippers.

Jess picked up as many tiny creatures
as possible, and ran to a nearby hill with

her arms full of trembling hamsters, voles, mice and baby hedgehogs.

Lily and Goldie ran around giving pushes to kittens, squirrels and bunnies in rubber rings, sending them bobbing towards safety.

 47

Those on high ground huddled
together, watching the water rise.
Everyone looked horrified.

Jess said quietly, "Friendship Forest is on
the other side of Shimmer Lake. It must
be flooding there, too."

Lily gasped. "Let's call for the butterflies
so they can warn the animals."

The butterflies carried messages around
the forest. To summon them, the girls put
their hands together then opened and
closed them, just like butterfly wings.
But when they looked up, they didn't see
butterflies flying towards them – instead,

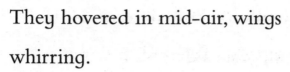

they saw three
dragonflies!

They hovered in mid-air, wings
whirring.

"Hello," said one with shimmering
silvery wings. His voice was like tiny
leaves rustling. "I'm Danny Dartwing."

"Hello!" said Lily. "But where are the
butterflies?"

"Butterflies don't carry messages on
Sapphire Isle," said Danny. "We

dragonflies do

that. How can

we help?"

Jess explained that the water levels of the lake were rising dangerously. "Please tell the animals to climb trees or get to high ground," she said.

"On our way!" chorused the dragonflies, zooming off.

"We've done what we can to keep the animals safe," said Lily. "Now we must stop that flood."

Amy looked helplessly at the two girls. "How?"

"There's only one way," Jess said. "We must find that sapphire."

CHAPTER FOUR

Butterfly Fish

"Let's borrow Admiral Greatwing's map!" Lily said. "It will show us where the sapphire is!"

Admiral Greatwing the albatross lived in a ship on a hill in the middle of the island. His magical map showed where the four sapphires were. If a sapphire moved, its symbol on the map moved, too.

But Goldie shook her head. "The map only shows the sapphires when they're above ground. This one's underwater!"

Lily looked at the waves slapping over the beach wall. "Then we must go underwater, too!"

Amy clapped her flippers excitedly. "I'll come!" she said. "I'll help you stay safe in the rough water. I'm a really strong swimmer."

She rushed to where Mr Snowycoat was drying off other animals, and soon returned. "Dad says yes, and Mr

Cleverfeather is bringing us something to help! Here he comes!"

The elderly owl was carrying a net holding three round objects. He flapped his wings hard as he came in to land, then flopped to the ground. "Oof! Here are the hubble beds," he puffed.

"He means the bubble heads!" Goldie said delightedly.

 53

"Thanks, Mr Cleverfeather," said Lily. "They'll make swimming underwater much easier!"

Amy looked puzzled.

"It's Mr Cleverfeather's invention!" Jess explained. "They are magical helmets that make you able to breathe and talk underwater. We borrowed them when we got the Paddlefoots' sapphire back from Grizelda's imps."

They put on the helmets and the four friends climbed onto the beach wall. Amy slipped into the rough water, then Jess, Lily and Goldie followed.

Although they'd used the bubble heads before, they were still amazed that they could breathe and talk underwater when they were wearing them.

"Where do we start?" Amy asked, streaking around them.

"The imps used an underwater cave last time they stole a sapphire," said Lily. "Maybe that's where they've gone. It's this way."

They set off down through the churning lake but were soon struggling. Twice, Goldie tumbled over and over, but the girls grabbed her, holding her close.

"The current's too strong," said Jess.

Amy glided over. "Use your arms like this!" She showed them how she used her flippers to pull herself through the water. "You haven't got tails, so kick your legs really hard."

Goldie and the girls did as she said, and found it much easier moving through the water.

"You're a good teacher," said Lily.

Amy smiled. "I love teaching."

Goldie suddenly pointed with her paw. "Something's coming!"

What looked like a brightly coloured

 57

cloud hurtled towards them.

"Is it the imps?" cried Lily.

"No!" said Jess. "It's a shoal of fish!"

The fish were patterned in bright,

shimmering colours, and had long

fluttering fins.

"They're butterfly fish!" said Amy. "And

they look scared!"

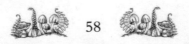

The colourful creatures swam between the friends, and hovered with quivering fins.

"What's wrong?" asked Jess.

"We're s-swimming away f-from some

w-water imps," said an orange and blue fish. His voice fluttered, like his fins. "They f-frightened us."

"Do you know where they went?" Lily asked hopefully. "They've stolen a sapphire. If we can get it back we can help save the lake."

"They w-went t-towards the C-Coral Forest," said the butterfly fish.

"I know where that is!" said Amy.

"We'll sort those imps out," Jess told the fish, "so you don't need to be scared any more."

"Thanks for your help," Lily added.

The friends swam away.

Soon, Amy stopped at the top of an underwater cliff. Lily and Jess peered over the edge and gasped.

A maze of sandy pathways twisted through jewel-bright coral. Some of it was shaped like trees, some like flowery bushes, some like toadstools and some like tall pillars. Weak sunlight filtered through the swirling water, creating changing patterns of colour.

"The Coral Forest!" said Amy.

"It's beautiful!" said Lily. "And it's a perfect hiding place."

"But how will we ever find four tiny imps in all that coral?" said Goldie. "The forest is enormous!"

"Well," said Jess, "we won't find them –
or the sapphire – if we don't try!"

"You're right," said Lily. "We have to at
least have a go!"

"Then follow me," said Amy. She dived
towards the Coral Forest.

CHAPTER FIVE

Stella Silverlegs

Goldie and the girls followed, but strong currents still pulled them this way and that. They copied Amy's movements, pushing their arms forward and pulling back hard. It felt like crawling through a muddy field, but it worked!

Once they reached the Coral Forest,

Amy said, "There's nobody here! Where are all the forest creatures?"

"Maybe they swam away to escape the currents," Goldie suggested.

They searched for the sapphire through coral of every colour. Jess and Lily felt as if they were swimming through a dream. Beneath little trees of coral were tiny round coral cottages, with names over the doors. The first one said "Kevin Clackershell", with a picture of a cheeky

little crab.
The next
cottage
had eight
pink shoes

on the windowsill. Above the door was a

picture of a pretty octopus and the words,

"Tina Tippytapper, Dance Lessons".

They knocked on the door to ask if

anyone had seen the imps, but there was

no one home.

Suddenly, Jess spotted something blue. "Over here!" she shouted. "I think it's the sapphire!"

But it was just blue coral.

A golden glint caught Lily's eye. It was a medal dangling from a coral tube. "The imps have definitely been here!" she said.

"They're not here now," Amy said sadly.

A clear voice said, "I'm glad they're not."

Goldie glanced around. "Who was that?"

Lily pointed. "It came from that little yellow cottage."

They swam over and found a beautiful silvery starfish clinging to the doorway. She wore a red coral anklet on each of her five legs.

"Do you need help?" asked Goldie.

"No, thanks," said the starfish. "I'm just being careful not to get swept away. The lake's in a terrible state!"

"That's why we're here," said Jess. "What's your name?"

"Stella," the starfish replied. With one of her five legs,

she pointed to a sign above her door. It said, "Stella Silverlegs, Jeweller".

"I'm the only creature left in the forest," she continued. "My legs are strong, so I can avoid getting swished away. But I've never seen you before! Who are you?"

The four of them introduced themselves and explained what they were looking for.

"Those imps tore through our forest!" the starfish said. "They were very shouty!" She pointed with one of her legs again. "They went that way."

"Thanks!" said Goldie and the girls, but

they noticed that Amy had gone quiet.

"What's wrong?" Stella asked kindly.

"The Deep Dark Depths are that way," said Amy. "Dad says that it's so dark down there, you can't see anything. We'd never spot a little sapphire."

"Wait," said Stella. She inched into her cottage and shut the door. A moment later she appeared at the window, holding four brightly glowing pearl bracelets. "These will help you see."

The four friends thanked Stella and put on the bracelets.

"We'll do our best to calm the water,"

Lily promised, as they swam away.

The deeper they went, the harder it was to see each other. They were glad of the bracelets lighting their way.

Soon, the pearly glow showed sharp rocks just ahead, so they turned aside.

"It's even darker now!" cried Lily. "Don't lose your bracelets!"

Then, without warning – *whoosh!* They were swept along by a strong, swirling current. Jess and Lily tumbled over and over, as if they'd been caught in a whirlpool.

"Help!" Jess cried in fright. "We're heading for the rocks!"

CHAPTER SIX

The Deep Dark Depths

"Hold on to me!" came Amy's voice. "I'll keep you off the rocks!"

The girls and Goldie grabbed her flippers as they hurtled downwards. The current whizzed them through the water. Seaweed flashed past, and Jess grabbed on

 71

tight to her bubble head to stop it from flying off. At last, they felt the current slow, and they were in calm water again – but it was still as black as a moonless night!

"This must be the Deep Dark Depths," said Amy, her voice shivering.

By holding the four bracelets together, there was enough light to see a little way in front of them. It glinted on huge jagged rocks standing all around.

Lily noticed a cave opening in the rocks. Keeping close together, they swam towards it and peered inside.

By the light of the bracelets, they could just make out Shrimp sitting against the wall! And something around his neck glinted in the pearly light.

"He's wearing the medals!" Jess whispered.

The other imps were huddled at the back of the cave. Something

blue and sparkly glimmered in the gloom.

Lily gasped. "I think Barnacle's holding the sapphire!"

Amy looked at the girls hopefully. "Can we get it?"

"Yes," Jess said firmly. "We've got them cornered. I'm going straight in to tell them to give it back."

Holding her pearly bracelet high, she led the others inside.

The imps stared, shocked, at Jess in her bubble head.

"That sapphire doesn't belong to you," she said. "Give it back."

All four imps said, "No!"

Then Goldie asked sternly, "Have you noticed how worried and frightened all the animals are?"

The imps shrugged and looked away.

"It's mean to ruin their homes," said Lily. "Give us the sapphire and we'll put things right."

The imps shook their heads.

"They're so quiet," Jess whispered. "Why aren't they shouting, as usual?"

"They're trembling," Lily said. "Maybe they're scared!"

"What of?" asked Amy.

Lily turned to the imps. "What's wrong?" she asked. "Maybe we can help."

Kelp looked at the others. "Shall we tell them, mateys?" he asked in a worried voice. The other imps nodded.

"This is how it be," he said. "We loves the water, but Grizelda's made it scary."

"Aye," said Barnacle. "Us be too small for strong currents."

"It be too dark," said Urchin. "My tummy's rumbling and there be no—"

"Hush up, Urchin," said Shrimp.

"Give us the sapphire," said Jess. "We'll calm the water and help you out of the Deep Dark Depths."

Kelp peered at the girls. "Be that the truth?"

"We promise," said Lily.

Kelp reached for the sapphire, but Barnacle put it behind her back. "Avast!" she said. "If you gives it to the girls, Grizelda will be angry and we won't get the ship she promised us!"

Urchin snorted. "Us couldn't sail it in nasty, choppy water like this, anyway."

"Forget Grizelda," said Jess. "You know we can beat her! Just give the sapphire back, and everything will be right again."

Barnacle frowned, thinking hard. Then, very slowly, she drew the sapphire out from behind her back and handed it over.

Lily fished the blue shell from her pocket, and Amy placed the sapphire inside. It gleamed softly in the pearly light.

"Let's leave this place," said Goldie.

The four friends swam up to the cave entrance, followed by the imps. Cautiously, they all peered out.

The swirling water was calming down.

 78

"Shimmer Lake's returning to normal," said Jess. "We can swim back up."

The imps looked nervous.

"I be frighted to swim back," Shrimp said. "It be dark!"

Amy smiled at him. "If we keep together," she said, "we can do it! I'll show you what we do in my swimming lessons. Everyone, get into a circle and hold hands, paws and flippers."

They did so. Jess held Barnacle's tiny rough hand and Goldie's furry paw. Lily held Amy's soft flipper while Shrimp's little hand clutched hers tightly.

"On 'go'," said Amy, "kick off as hard as you can, and keep kicking. Ready?"

They nodded.

"GO!" cried Amy.

Flippers, paws and legs kicked off! The circle of friends shot up through the water, towards the light above.

 80

CHAPTER SEVEN

The Swimming Gala

The circle of swimmers burst through the surface near the Sapphire Isle.

Amy turned a joyful somersault, while the others cheered.

After lots of giggles, the imps broke into song.

"We be four little imps,

As happy as can be!

Thanks to our new friends,

We're glad we is free!"

"Fluffy, matey," Kelp said to Amy, "we thank ye."

"And we thank the girls and the cat," said Barnacle.

"We be off to hunt treasure!" said Shrimp.

"And cook sea biscuits!" said Urchin. "My tummy be rumbling like a growling walrus!"

"Goodbye!" called Jess.

"Don't worry about Grizelda!" cried

Lily, as the imps swam away. "She's nothing but a meanie."

The water was almost back to its normal level, and lots of animals were heading for the beach, cheering!

Mr Snowycoat swam out to meet the friends, with Jack on his back.

"You did it!" he said, as they headed to shore.

"Diddit!" said Jack.

Mr Snowycoat took the sapphire. "We need a better

hiding place," he said. "Grizelda must never get her hands on this again."

Jess's feet touched the bottom, so she stood up. "I know the perfect hiding place," she said. "The Deep Dark Depths!"

"Ooh, yes!" said Amy. "Now I've been there, I won't be scared anymore!"

Lily grinned. "If you decorate the cave with our pearly bracelets, it will look quite pretty!"

Mr Snowycoat decided to hide the sapphire right away. "When I get back," he said, "we'll start the swimming gala."

Amy was so excited she turned a

double somersault! "Whoopee!"

★

Once the warm sunshine had dried
everywhere out, it was gala time!

Jess, Lily and Goldie wandered around,
greeting friends. Katie Prettywhiskers
waved from the Prettywhiskers' Purrfect
Ice Cream Parlour. Millie Picklesnout
the piglet was sitting on a rug with her
family, wrapped in a hooded towel.
"I'm in the underwater race!" she yelled.
"Watch me!"

"Definitely!" Jess called.

Admiral Greatwing the albatross beckoned Goldie and the girls over. He was sitting in a creaking deckchair, with a picnic spread out beside him. "Do join me," he said.

"Thanks!" they replied. As they sat, two seagull chicks flew down.

"Skye and Marina Saltybill!" Jess said.

Marina hugged her.

"Grandma Gail

brought us to the gala," she said.

Skye hopped onto Lily's lap. "It's exciting seeing everyone," she said. "The Brightbeak puffins are here, too."

"So they are!" Goldie giggled, as Pedro, Jade and little Roxy Brightbeak flew past, doing roly-polies in the air.

Amy hurried across. "Look who's here!" she said, pointing a flipper.

The four imps waved from the top of a sandcastle! They had a net full of shiny shells.

"These be to decorate our treasure chest," Barnacle shouted.

"When we gets one!" said Kelp.

A whistle blew. It was Mr Snowycoat, from his podium.

The backstroke race started again. Molly Twinkletail's sister, Dolly, won, and celebrated by doing somersaults through the water. The rest of the mouse family went wild with excitement, squeaking and hopping up and down.

No one could see what was happening in the underwater race, so Amy bobbed down to look, then kept bobbing up to shout, "Mrs Greenshell's in the lead!" or "Millie Picklesnout's catching up!" In the

end, the first swimmer to pop up at the finishing line was Phoebe Paddlefoot!

Halfway through the gala, the Flippershell turtles performed a special swimming display. They marched into the water, wearing swimming hats in different colours. Mr Flippershell, wearing red, called, "Rainbow formation! Go!"

They lined up – red, orange, yellow, green, blue, indigo and little Violet at the end, then formed a circle. First they went head down, tails up, then they floated on their backs, waving their flippers in the air.

Jess and Lily cheered as the turtles

ducked and dived, spinning and
swimming, with the little hats making
colourful patterns in the water. Finally,
the Flippershells turned on their sides and
swam off, each waving a flipper at the
cheering spectators.

When all the races were over, Mr
Snowycoat presented medals to the
winners, and everyone had an ice cream
from the Prettywhiskers' parlour.

"Congratulations to all our winners!"
said Mr Snowycoat. "Now, I've got four
more very special medals to present. Lily,
Jess, Goldie and Amy, please could you

come up to the podium?"

They went and stood beside him. The crowd of animals smiled up at them.

"You all protected Shimmer Lake," Mr Snowycoat told them, "and saved the Sapphire Isle!"

He put a medal around Amy's neck

and gave her a big hug.

"Thanks, Dad!" she said, as all the

animals cheered in delight.

Then he asked Goldie and the girls to kneel down while he hung medals around their necks.

"Thanks!" they said, thrilled. They hugged each other in delight, but stopped when the spectators' cheers turned to frightened shouts.

The lake was churning again!

As they stared, a slimy, seaweed-covered ship rose out of the water. Its flag had a cauldron and crossed brooms.

Jess and Lily gasped. "Grizelda!"

CHAPTER EIGHT

A Gift for the Imps

The frightened animals huddled under deckchairs and behind the ice cream parlour. Several tiny ones scurried to Admiral Greatwing.

Grizelda's hatch opened, out of it her thin, bony face appeared. It was purple with fury.

Her green hair blew in the breeze like grubby streamers. "You wicked girls! You horrible cat! You nasty little seal!" she screamed. "You've ruined my plan to take over the Sapphire Isle." She glared at the water imps. "And you!"

The imps clutched each other, shaking with terror.

"You're useless!" Grizelda screeched. "But you'll be sorry!" She shook her fists. "You're not getting a ship now!"

The poor imps looked very upset.

Grizelda raged on, stamping and shaking her fists. She stamped so hard

that the steamboat started rocking.

Suddenly, she slipped. Her legs flew up in the air, and over the side she went.

Splash!

The animals stared in shock.

"Come on, Lily!" cried Jess. "Grizelda needs help!"

Amy had already thrown Grizelda a rubber ring. As the witch grabbed it and put it over her head, the little seal pup

 95

dived into the lake and swam to her.

Lily and Jess splashed towards the struggling Grizelda. They gripped her bony arms and, with Amy's help, pulled her ashore. She sat, spluttering.

"You should learn to swim," said Amy. "I could teach you, if you like?"

"No!" Grizelda snapped.

Kelp peered from behind Jess. "We be friends with the girls, Grizelda. They did help you, so you should be friends, too."

"No chance!" Grizelda roared. "I've had enough of the silly Sapphire Isle, I've had enough of you lot, and I'm never getting on a boat again!" Water dripped from her chin. "But, watch out. I'll be back. One day I'll take over Friendship Forest, and you'll all be GONE!"

She snapped her fingers and then she disappeared, in a final shower of stinky yellow sparks.

After a moment's surprised silence, the loudest cheer rang out!

"Hooray!"

The animals jumped for joy and the imps did a sailors' hornpipe dance. They didn't do it very well and ended up having a little squabble.

 97

Jess realised that the witch's steamboat was still on the lake – empty. "Grizelda seems to have deserted her boat," she said to Lily.

They grinned and called the imps over.

Kelp, Barnacle and Shrimp were first. Urchin stopped to grab a strawberry doughnut from Admiral Greatwing's picnic.

"You imps can have a ship after all," Lily said. "I don't think Grizelda wants it any more."

The imps did their dance again, shouting for joy!

"Hooray for the girls!"

"Hooray for Amy!"

"Hooray for Goldie!

Then they chorused, "And boo for Grizelda!"

When Lily reminded them that the steamboat would even go underwater, they were speechless with delight.

Then Kelp frowned.

"What's up?" asked Amy.

"It don't be looking like a pirate ship," he said.

Goldie grinned. "We can put that right. Just watch!"

*

Lily helped the Paddlefoots to paint the steamboat black. Mr Cleverfeather had used his Hover Workshop to rig up sails, while Jess and Amy made a pirate flag to flutter from the mast.

Goldie painted *Treasure Seeker* on the side. The imps were thrilled. "We'll never harm Friendship Forest again!" they said.

"We be off to hunt for treasure!"

Everyone waved as they sailed away. Then Jess said to Lily, "It's time to go home."

Amy was sad, but they promised to come back again soon.

"You've really improved our swimming!" said Lily. "Perhaps we could explore the Coral Forest next time?"

"I'd love to," said Amy. "Bye, Jess and Lily. Bye, Goldie!"

Mr Cleverfeather took them across the lake in his boat, back to the forest.

"I hope you'll be sack boon," he said.

"We hope so, too!" Jess smiled.

"Goodbye, and thanks!" said Lily.

Goldie took the girls to the Friendship Tree. She touched a paw to the trunk, and the little door appeared.

"Grizelda's sure to return," she said, hugging them. "When she does, Friendship Forest will need your help."

"We'll be ready," Lily promised. "Goodbye, Goldie."

They stepped through the door into shimmering golden light. When the light faded, they found themselves back in Brightley Meadow.

 102

"What a fantastic adventure!" Jess said, as they ran back to Helping Paw.

Lily realised they still had their medals on. "Better put these in our pockets," she said. "No one would believe we got them for saving a magical island from a witch!"

Jess laughed.

Just then, Mrs Hart came out of the barn with a box. Inside were some small wriggling terrapins.

"Their owner moved away, so they need a new home," she said. "They'll love living in our new pond!"

The girls helped launch them into the

water, then watched as the tiny terrapins swam around happily.

Jess whispered, "They love swimming as much as Amy!"

Lily giggled. "And it looks like they're having their very own swimming gala!"

The girls watched the terrapins, who seemed to be having just as much fun as the animals in Friendship Forest. The girls couldn't wait to go back there for their next adventure.

The End

Lily and Jess can't wait for Christmas in Friendship Forest! But when wicked witch Grizelda turns up on her sleigh, the festive plans are in trouble. Can little puppy Holly Santapaws help save the day?

Find out in the next adventure,

Holly Santapaws
Saves Christmas

Turn over for a sneak peek . . .

"Shoo!" Lily Hart chased two wild geese away from her mum's cabbage plants. Her best friend, Jess Forester, helped guide the greedy birds to the Harts' new pond.

Nearby was the Helping Paw Wildlife Hospital, which Lily's parents ran in a barn in their garden. The poorly animals were inside, but those who were getting better were in pens outside enjoying fresh air.

Winter sunlight shone through bare trees, making spiky shadows on the grass. Mrs Hart was putting out bowls of juicy lettuce and crunchy carrots for bunnies, guinea pigs and tortoises to enjoy.

"Offer the geese this," she said, handing the girls some spinach and lettuce. "That will keep them off my veggies. It's turning colder, so they'll soon be flying off to somewhere warmer."

"Will they go together?" asked Jess.

Mrs Hart nodded. "A pair of geese are partners for life," she said with a smile, as she wondered away to feed some baby badgers.

"Like being married!" Lily whispered.

The girls shared a smile as they

watched the geese eagerly tucking into the leaves.

"We'll soon be going to a real wedding in Friendship Forest," Jess said excitedly.

Lily slipped a white card from her pocket. It was leaf-shaped, and decorated with frosted silver bells. It read,

"You are invited to
the winter wedding of
Mr Cleverfeather to Miss Sweetbeak
in Silver Glade, Friendship Forest
and to a celebration at the
Toadstool Café."

Lily laughed. "Whoever thought we'd see two owls get married!"

Read

Holly Santapaws
Saves Christmas

to find out what happens next!

Jess and Lily's Animal Facts

Lily and Jess love lots of different animals –
both in Friendship Forest
and in the real world.

Here are their top facts about

SEALS

like Amy Snowcoat:

- Seals spend most of their lives in the sea, and can
  even sleep underwater.

- Seals mostly eat fish, though some species also
  eat squid, birds and penguins.

- The world's most endangered seal is the Saimaa
  ringed seal from Finland.

- The Baikal seal is the smallest seal at 1.1 to 1.4 metres
  long. The largest is the male elephant seal, which can
  reach a length of 6.5 metres!

Can you keep the secret?

There's lots of fun for everyone at
www.magicanimalfriends.com

Play games and explore the secret world of
Friendship Forest, where animals can talk!

Join the
Magic Animal Friends Club!

✶ Special competitions ✶
✶ Exclusive content ✶
✶ All the latest Magic Animal Friends news! ✶

To join the Club, simply go to

www.magicanimalfriends.com/join-our-club/